Left to Wr!te

An anthology of works

by

Manningtree Library Writers Group

ISBN: 1983775703
ISBN-13: 978-1983775703

PREFACE

Outside the library a big notice;

'Do you fancy doing some creative writing? If so, come inside and sign up.'

As easy as that several of us applied and on a Thursday afternoon in June 2017 we all met at the library. Margherita sat poised to share her knowledge with us and so we began.

With a mish mash of writing styles, we all listened as we each read our work aloud and gradually, we settled into a friendly, organised group. Writing exercises stretched our pens and homework focused our ideas.

As the little pieces increased, the idea of a book formed and so you have before you, a selection of very different work which somehow all flows together.

So please take the time to read the stories and poems from this group of budding authors. Laugh, cry or just listen to what we have to say, but most of all, enjoy!

ACKNOWLEDGEMENTS

Our thanks go to the librarians at Manningtree library, especially Mandy and Angela, for their continued help and support

Contents

DEDICATION

Dedicated with love to Alan Arnold, one of our founder members..

Bookworm

My Life in Libraries

by
Jude Hussey

Long ago, in the faraway land of childhood, my first library was the book-shelf collection that took up the corner of my parent's smart new council flat.

In an early photo, I must be about three years old, I can be seen showing the photographer my latest choice from that library! We cannot see the book's title but my parents belonged to a book club and often bought the monthly title on offer.

I believe this was quite common in those days as occasionally these books still turn up in charity shops, in good condition as they were nicely bound hard-backs.

Nothing was more exciting than scrutinizing the cover of a new book and tentatively turning the pages. What did these strange marks on the page mean? The next step was to trail round the adults until I found someone to translate for me!

Usually, it was Dad that lifted me onto his lap and read the selected text, running his fore-finger under the words as he did so. Much later, I realised that this was how I had learnt to read, long before I started school.

By then, I had read the usual children's books available to me. Mainly, Enid Blyton, Fairy Tales and nursery rhymes. I had a treasured volume of Robert Louis Stevenson's A Child's Garden of Verses that Auntie had bought me. My favourite poem being The Lamplighter, as Dad told me that he could remember the lamplighters lighting the street lamps before the war.

Infant school was a huge disappointment. Just a small class library and a strange reading scheme, relating the boring lives of Dick and Dora with their pets Nip and Fluff!

This is Dick. Run Dick run. Nip is a dog. Run to Dick. See Dora run! See Judith run! All the way home one day! No Happy Venture for me!

I was bored, bored, bored and polished off the class library in no time.

Around this time I was introduced to my first public library, very close to my second home, which was a brand new council 'Semi'. The small library was housed in a temporary building, which was also the premise of the local evening classes. For this small bibliophile it seemed like a perfect world and I would happily taken up residence! Just to lose myself in the pages of all those books…

I began to devour the feast on offer, welcoming into my life Milly Molly Mandy, Mary Poppins, The Family from One End Street, The Famous Five et al!

My life was my local library and it was just at the bottom of the road, just pedal furiously until you reached the small building attached to the further education annexe. For now, I had a small bicycle, my trusty Raleigh with a saddle-bag, big enough to hold my treasured library books.

Oh Joy!

Not so my first encounter with A Librarian! He was the archetypal grumpy old git. I was a bit scared of Mr. Green but I would watch closely, on tiptoe, as he placed the ticket from my chosen book into my very own reader's pocket with my name on and stamped the book with the return date.

I wondered how Mr. Green would find it when I returned

the books but later he explained about alphabetical order and I was fascinated all over again! I think I was allowed two books at a time but it was never enough and I would return hungrily in a couple of days for my next two.

By this time Mr. Grumpy and I were best of friends and sometimes I was allowed to 'shelve' the books. You see, I was very impressed with this alphabetical order business and couldn't get enough. Now I could show dad how to organise his books in those bookcases at home. I spent many happy hours ordering the family collection.

As you might guess, the library only had a limited selection of books and I soon read my way through the titles on offer.

How I pleaded to be let loose in the adult section. I suppose it was just before secondary school. It didn't take me long to find her, tucked away among the Bs, as I always traversed the shelves alphabetically of course.

Jane Eyre! How I loved that poor orphan girl's story and I went on to discover the Brontes and their world of wild moors and lost souls.

If it hadn't been for Mr. Grumpy, I may not have found her so easily. I know that Jane Eyre inspired the writing of my first real story, The Red Room, written in my final year at primary school. Mr. Grumpy was now promoted to Guru!

Then he was gone! On arriving at my library one evening it was padlocked and in darkness. I checked the opening times on the door. No, I hadn't got the wrong time. My world stopped turning as I cycled home confused and worried.

Little did I know that my little library had grown and taken up residence in a brand new building! I had much further to pedal now but it was 1960 and I was at the local high school so this was allowed.

The famous poet, John Betjeman, opened this beautiful new public library. I found some of my old friends on the shelves upstairs in the children's section. Dozens of shelves with lots of new books but I could browse freely now in the adult section downstairs. My first visit lasted for hours and I was issued with four books! I had four fresh new pink pockets too! There was a desk big enough for two librarians to stamp the books!

There were arm- chairs to curl up in with a book and desks to look up homework stuff. There was a non-fiction section which seemed to be organised in a different way from the fiction. I had discovered Mr. Dewey!

I was almost at one with the world, but not quite. I wondered what had happened to Mr. Grumpy. It was not until I joined the wonderful life of librarians myself, at 18, and I was despatched upstairs to do some filing in the long and narrow aisles of the 'stack', where all old and battered books were retired that I found out! I could hear the faint clicketty - clacking of a typewriter and I cautiously made my way towards it.

I tip-toed round the last tall shelves and there he was; hunched over a desk, at the far end of the stack; his now-greying head bent over his work was my Mr. Grumpy! I introduced myself and do you know what?

He smiled and put out his hand to shake mine. I was home!

Another Christmas

by
Carol Cordwell

The wrapping paper lay bunched up on the floor. The excitement of opening the present was no more. An empty box lay on its side, no longer the gift to hide.

The elderly lady jigged around, her bottom wobbling to the sound, of the music from the headphones that vibrated right through her bones.

It wouldn't last long, her energy spent, she went and sat down in her chair, enjoying the rest it gave her there.

A tear rolled down her cheek, from her family not a peep! they had other things to do and hadn't seen that she was blue.

The table laid, the tree all pretty, lots of food to fill them up.

By now it was cold, all dried up, the burnt down candles, the unopened crackers.

She could have gone away with her friend but she wanted to stay home, she thought of her family and waited by her phone.

When she realised they wouldn't come, she indulged on Christmas cake, ate lots of chocolates and binged on dates.

A few cards adorned the walls, some tinsel decorated the hall. Well now it was over and just as before, she sat and waited and stared at the door.

Tomorrow she would put the decorations away, clear up the food, and begin a new day.

Her friends would be calling to check she was fine, ask about her Christmas and then she would lie; "It was a last minute thing, they all got held up, they will try and visit in spring. My present must have got lost in the post, it doesn't mean anything. I've put theirs in the cupboard just until they come, except for the headphones, I'm going to keep that one."

Her friends looked on sadly, she did this every year, the rest of the time she was filled with cheer.

Her family had died several years before, they had crashed on a snowy road out on the moor. All of them had died; parents and one son. They had never arrived, they had never come.

So every year she did this, pretending they were still alive. So sad that it had happened, over Christmas time.

They had been on their way to see her, they loved her oh so much! They had always been on the phone, always kept in touch.

Normally she could accept it, but just for a few days, she could pretend they were still on their way.

But this year it was different, she couldn't do it anymore, she had to stop pretending, accept they couldn't come.

She didn't decorate for Christmas, she didn't buy any food. At long last she was going with her friend on a Christmas Cruise.

She had visited the graveyard and said her long goodbyes, the tears had run down her cheeks as she cried and cried.

She wouldn't visit here again, it really was too sad. She would just remember the happy times and for them she was very glad!

.

Missed Connection

by
Margherita Petrie

Having boarded the wrong train at Liverpool Street Station, Maria was shocked when at the end of her journey she found herself stranded at a strange station. The porter at Liverpool Street must have told her the wrong platform where she was to pick up the connecting train bound for Colchester. An icy wind whistled down the deserted, litter strewn platform as she despairingly watched the departing train noisily disappear into the distance.

"You're too late for the last train to Colchester Mam," an elderly man in the shabby uniform of a station master called out as he disappeared through a side gate.

"But ....." it was useless, he was gone.

She was suddenly filled with fear as a lone figure loomed up out of the darkness. It had started to snow. She wanted to run, but to where? Struggling with her cases, which seemed to have become even heavier, Maria found herself weak with cold and fatigue.

The lone figure, though motionless, was still visible through the now heavily falling snow.

The only light appeared to be coming from what she thought must be the waiting room. Now safely inside the dimly lit small room, containing two scruffy armchairs and a ring marked table, on which she placed one of her cases; Maria searched for something warm to wrap around her shivering body. Wrapped in her fleece dressing gown and saying a silent prayer of thanks for her grandmother's parting gifts of her home cheese scones and bar of chocolate, she tried to settle herself by the dwindling coke fire. Looking worriedly over at the door, wishing it had a lock, she thought of the lone figure. Who was he? Why was he out there? Would he want to come inside out of the cold? Could it be a woman and like herself, stranded for the night? She dozed; suddenly awakened from her fitful slumbers by the distant sound of a train whistle. The heavy air was filled with a mixture of smoke and steam as she boarded the ancient vehicle. The carriage was full of seemingly faceless people, all dressed in black as though returning from a funeral. A strange odour filled the air.

"What Train is this?" Maria's voice nervously broke into the hushed silence.

"This is the last connecting train."

Fact, Fiction or In Between

by
Hester Kenneison 2018

The sky is shading towards darkness when she heads home. There's light along the horizon, tinting it blue-edged-with-gold but the clouds above are a streak of shadow already carrying night in their wake. Beneath her, her moped struggles up the last stretch of hill, chugging a little, but managing.

Beyond bare hedges the fields spread far away. In the facing light some twigs, some strands of grass, carry the slight rime of ice. Even with her helmet and jacket the wind is pointedly cold.

Out of the hedges, out of the shadows, a fragment of darkness takes form.

It stays out of the lights of her moped, loping along moving in odd see-saw as the light hits and casts shadows here and there. On level ground her moped speeds up, chugs less. The shadow keeps loping pace with ease.

She can't see it, not easily. It's a shadow, inherently without form and while the horizon shines with light the skies above are dark and darkening, the bare trees and high earthen banks build boundaries around her.

Beside her shadowed-shuck lopes on.

She can see his legs, but not his claws, can see his tail but not his fur. She can see his head but not his eyes. Not the sharp snapping teeth that await her in his jaws.

It is not the wind that makes her shiver now.

She drives on, drives faster around ice-dew slicked bends. She doesn't come off, but it's close. Shuck chases at her heels, shivers fear down her neck, makes her pant in desperation to flee until her visor is so fogged she almost misses the shadow lunging out of the hedgerows.

She brakes, twists the handlebars, almost falls over, gasping in bare terror.

But it's just a Muntjac.

Bert and Flora

by
Carol Cordwell

'Two big seagulls, standing on a wall,
One with long legs and one with small!'

'Will you please shut up flora?' snapped Bert. 'I am trying to concentrate. Ever since Peter and Paul taught you the new version of their rhyme, you repeat it constantly. Can I never have any peace?'

Flora looked into Bert's beady black eyes,

'Well, NO, I like it and I want to say it again!

Flora repeated the verse knowing that Bert was not happy. She could see him stretching his wings and craning his neck up to the sky, but when she saw the black eyes turn towards her with a malicious glint in them, she swallowed and closed her long yellow beak.

'What do you need to concentrate on Bert, it must be important.'

Flora sidled closer to Bert on the smooth seawall. It was a windy day and the waves of the sea crashed against the rocks behind them. Every now and then some water would shoot into the air and drop onto their feathers, like now. Flora shook her wing and waited for Bert to reply.

'I'm hungry,' said Bert, *'but there aren't many people about. Do you remember when they used to feed us and smile about it? I can recall soaring in the sky and then gliding down to where someone was eating. Easy pickings my girl, easy pickings.'*

Flora sighed, she had heard it all before. She could

11

remember those days which seemed so long ago. Gulping down the food as quickly as it was thrown down Flora had often over indulged, then with a heavy tummy she would fly off onto a distant rock to digest her prize. Bert turned his head to see who was about. He was a large gull, his white feathers kept in pristine condition. After all, he had to look good for the crowds.

'It's not fair, now that no one is encouraged to feed us, its slim pickings. I never thought that I would have to start pulling wrappers out of the bins to get enough to eat. The indignity of it all! Why the other day I ate a sauce wrapper, a sauce wrapper!'

'Why did you do that Bert?' Flora questioned.

'I thought it was a sausage didn't I. It made me feel right queer,' Flora started talking again.

'People were worried that we were getting too aggressive and scaring the children. Do you remember when Bill spied that ice cream from up on the lamppost. He took off and zoned in on that child, before they knew it the ice cream was gone and the child was crying."

Bert let Flora waffle on. It didn't matter what she said. The people had made the food so tasty. They were messy and threw it away without finishing it half the time They didn't deserve it. Why! Didn't he let them see him up close, give them a chance to admire his fine feathers. He ought to get something out of it. Walking up and down the wall he sighed, now he had to jump down and pick up a sparse chip or two dropped by somebody careless.

'Hold on Flora, I've just spotted a couple with some chips. Look over there.'

Bert could feel his stomach rumbling, *'I'm off!'* and before Flora could reply Bert was on his way. He flew towards the couple, circling over their heads. He screeched to draw their attention and as they looked up, he dived down towards the chips so fast that the couple dropped several in their rush to move away. Bert landed on the ground as the couple walked off cursing him. Quickly he gobbled down the chips, they hardly touched his throat as his beak shoveled them into his mouth. After circling round the area on his feet, Bert flew back to Flora.

'*That was fun,*' he said. Flora looked at Bert.

'*No wonder we have a bad name, was that necessary?*' Flora turned her head away from Bert and then she spied something edible by the bench. A shadow flew over her head, it was Bill and he was looking, looking over at the bench too.

'Oh *no you don't,*' said Flora and she shot off the wall to get to the food first. She briefly chased Bill who wasn't happy to see his chance for lunch disappearing. Flora landed and wolfed down the food, then she returned to Bert.
'*Happy now old girl?*' said Bert.

'Oh *yes,*' said Flora feeling nice and full. '*Two big seagulls, standing on a wall,*' Bert closed his eyes and ignored the annoying ditty.

Dexter

by
Roger Race

We had our first rescue cat approx. 9 years ago, he had been found on Half penny pier in Harwich and was suffering from pneumonia. We picked him up one snow laden night from a vet in Colchester and it was love at first sight. We named him Oskar and spoilt him rotten. Over the years, a lady who used to look after him whilst we were on holiday finally pursued us that he needed a playmate and sent us a picture of a grey and white fluffy cat that needed a home. We duly visited the foster carer and she introduced us to year old Dexter. Whilst agreeing that he looked cute, my mind set was that we were only getting him for Oskar`s benefit and that Oskar would always be number one. I had not realised that Dexter had other ideas and a clear game plan.

The first two months were challenging, as the two did not get on, much hissing, fights, and keeping them apart. We also had the problem of keeping Dexter in for the first month and as Dexter started to work his magic, were concerned that if they did not eventually get on we would have to take Dexter back. As time went on, they got used to each other and even played together. Dexter turned out to be a delight, the best natured cat we had ever had, unlike Oskar who when he was young could turn ferial at times. Dexter was so laid back that when things were too much he would just flop. He would sit on my lap with his legs up in the air and fall asleep. Whenever we arrived home, it would be Dexter who was the first one to greet us. Within a short period of time Dexter had turned from just a playmate to an equal first with Oskar. He found a den in the garden and if we could not find him at first, we knew where to look. We went away on a three- week holiday and the cats were looked after by our friend and by the time we got back, we were eager to see them. As soon as we got in, Oskar was waiting to greet us but no sign of Dexter. We were anxious but after an hour, Dexter finally decided to make an appearance, you could almost hear him say *"hey man chill out, what is the problem?"*

We had only been back a week when we received an early morning call from the vets. She had found Dexter by the side of a busy road, had been hit by a car and died instantly and she had taken him to the practice. We struggled to comprehend what she was saying, and I felt sick. We went down to the practice and she brought Dexter in, wrapped in a towel. He looked strangely peaceful and we cuddled him, reluctant to let go. Through tears we said goodbye to him. The next few days were a nightmare, although we had seen him, and the microchip confirmed it was him, it was difficult to accept that he had gone. Against all sense, I expected him to just come walking in though the backdoor, that it had not been him that we had identified, the vets had made a mistake with the microchip number. My emotions were a mixture of grief, sadness, despair, and of total anger. Anger that it had happened to us, anger that he was so young, and we had only had him for a year, anger that we had only been back a week, anger at the way some motorists treated the road like a racetrack.

We made extra fuss over Oskar, worried that he could be

stressed over Dexter, concerned to keep him safe.

In Dexter's den, we placed a lantern and candle. At night, the flickering flame seemed to keep the spirit of Dexter around, as if in some small way he was still with us. A week on and it still feels very raw, the house seems so empty without his big personality. Even Oskar has changed. Every morning without fail he would come up and see me before even eating, just to make sure that I was still here. This has changed, almost as if he blames me for the loss of his playmate. I wonder to myself how a parent copes with losing a child, if I feel like this over our cat, what must it be like for them; I cannot begin to understand how they would cope? I feel reluctant to lose the memory of Dexter but at the same time it feels the only way to get through this. We only had him for a short time, but he touched our hearts, RIP Dexter.

The Old Boot

By
Carol Cordwell

As I walked by a field I knew; I saw a shoe,
A toe stood out from the soil; where the tractor and the plough
had toiled.

The sun shone down to draw the eye; to the worn out shoe as I
passed by,
Where did it come from? What would I do? If I took pity on
this old brown shoe.

Several weeks later, it was still there; it lay in a rut amongst the crop,
Should I go and pick it up, sadly I did not.

What could I do with this old brown shoe; where did it come from, nobody knew,
I turned my back, I walked away; I forgot about it 'till that rainy day.

It was a few years later; I'd forgotten about the shoe,
When there in the road I saw it; in a puddle of dirty blue!
It couldn't be, surely not; the same shoe I had found,
Such a long time ago, in that muddy ground.

As I drove on past it; I seemed to hear it call,
You just cannot leave me; I need to tell you all.
As I went I ignored it; the voice inside my head,
Why was this shoe calling; because a shoe is really dead.

As I made my way home; I searched and looked along the road,
It lay where I last saw it; torn and battered and cold.
I picked it up, I don't why; It seemed to speak to me,
This inanimate object had a tale to tell; if only it would let me see.

This is the shoe I found on that day; flattened by time along the way,
Holey and battered; a sad old thing, left in the road to be shattered.
Wet and soggy I took it home; what should I do with it now?
I left it outside near the bins; a shiver ran over my brow.

The next day I was passing and there on my lounge chair,
I saw that soggy old brown shoe; who had put it there?
I picked it up and suddenly; suddenly I knew
It had a tale to tell me; this battered old brown shoe.

A haze filled the room; the roof disappeared and I could see the sky,
A black cloud went over and lightning forked up high.
A figure appeared before me; an old man battered and bruised,
'I was the one who wore them; I was the man with the shoes'.

'Who are you?' I shivered and trembled; what had happened to my house?
I stood now among some trees; as scared as a little grey mouse.
The man he spoke once again; the skies they opened, it began to rain
'You know where you are, you know the way; you see this wood most everyday'.

'It's Chequers Wood, but how? It looks nothing like this now'
'It wouldn't,' he said *'it couldn't be; we've gone back to 1943.'*
As I looked around I saw twas true; the trees were thick
The wind it blew and at my feet lay an old brown shoe.
'What do you want? What's this I see; I have to know, can't you tell me?
I'll listen, I will', the man looked at me and all went still.
'I was a vagrant, a hobo, a tramp; I wandered the country alone
My family were dead; I had no home.'

'It was during the war I came this way; I was looking for work on this day
At the last farm I had helped plant some fields and several meals it did yield.

19

At last the work had all dried up; I walked away to try my luck
I was tired and looked all about me; I lay my head down amongst these
trees.

I woke up in such a rush; there had been a roar and then a hush
I listened and looked into the sky; the night lit up and flashing by
A plane was dashing through the light; it looked on fire, it couldn't be!
That plane came crashing down on me!

It killed me here, right on this spot; they never ever found me,
As folks came rushing round to do all they could,
The wreckage of the plane lay all around the wood.'
My bones were crushed, quite overlooked and in the pouring rain
The blood and gore were washed away; never seen again.

I've been here such a long time; waiting here for you
Hoping someone would find; my spirit in the shoe.'
 What do you want?' I muttered, 'What has it to do with me?
Why didn't you ask someone else, why didn't you make them see?'

'*The time has come, I must now pass on'* the old man clearly said
I needed someone to know; how long that I've been dead.
My spirit is being called to go away and fly
But I can only do this; when someone knows I've died.'
My fear had left me long ago; my eyes were not quite dry
Just how could I help him? This person from the sky.

If you could tell my story; of how I came to die
The reason why you found the shoe and of this time gone by.
Of aeroplanes and thunderstorms; of what it once was like
Of where I was before; then tell them my name is.................'

But then a mighty roar rose up all around us; the trees they shook, the wind it blew
What on earth was happening? But I really knew.
All went still; a golden glow reached down from the sky
I saw it pick the old man up and take him way up high.

The next thing I knew; I was holding the shoe
The room was the same; the roof was back too.
I felt in shock; what had I seen?
How could I prove; that he had been?

I walked to the woods, much smaller now; I wandered and poked for many an hour
I hoped to find something to show he'd been there; that it wasn't a dream, I'd had in my chair.
 I couldn't see anything; it was so long ago,
The wood was still used; so I went very slow.

I went to see a farmer; Bromley born and bred
I didn't tell him about the shoe or of the man who was dead.

Instead I asked him; of the plane that had come down
'Did he know where it had landed? Where it had been found?'

A thoughtful look came into his eyes
He remembered the night; it flew through the skies
He was much younger than he is now
This Bromley farmer told me the tale;
'*A plane landed in Chequers Wood,*' I asked; he said '*No*' as he delved into the past,
 '*It landed in Wood Field; the next field on the right*
As it came down it clipped the trees, in the dead of night.'

'Were there any survivors? Was anyone hurt?
Was there lots of digging in the dirt?'
'Czech airmen, that's who survived; all of them were alive
They walked off down the road to the farm; none of them had come to
harm.'

All was clear, I knew it now; I wouldn't have found it anyhow,
I had been looking in the wrong place; so I set off at a pace.
The next day I went along to Wood Field
I hoped to find something; see what I might yield.
That's when I saw it, hidden in the root of the tree,
 Another brown shoe; looking at me!

It was the one of my pair I am sure
Because just as I touched it; it started to glow,
Just for a moment, it said Hello!
Then with a woosh! and a thundering sound; I felt the earth
shake, I fell to the ground.
The man reappeared; his head in the sky.
With a brilliant smile on his face; he said *'I knew you'd find the*
place'.

His hand flew down; he picked up the shoe
The rain it fell; the wind it blew.
I wandered home; I knew it was true and that I had the other
shoe.
So now I am telling you about this tramp; about this little old
Man, who died just because he happened to be tired,and laid
down by a tree;that was beside Chequers Wood; in Little
Bromley.

Romford Ray

by

Roger Race

The alarm went off with its high pitch wailing, desperately he fumbled, in the dark for the snooze button but gave up. He pulled back the curtains to reveal, through the grimy window, a dark dank sky overlooking East London. Raindrops pelted the window as if attempting to clean them from the outside. He reached for his first 'fag' of the day and let out a deep cough. Stumbling through the half light he went into the kitchen to put the kettle on.

This was Romford Ray or Raymondo to some of his friends. His real name was Hamidi, but nobody called him that, his parents were Turkish-Cypriot who had settled in England years ago. He had been born here, forty-two years ago and had an East London ascent. He was currently between girlfriends and was the father of two boys from different women to the despair of his mother. He had a fruit and veg stall on Romford market with another little money- making venture on the side. His home was a one-bed roomed high-rise council flat in East London.

He hated getting up early, but this was the nature of the market business. He was glad that he had loaded up the van last night, all he had to do was to load up his 'special box', this was too valuable to leave overnight. He finished his tea and got dressed, putting on his trademark leather jacket and making sure that he was also wearing his thick gold chain and sovereign ring. He got into the graffiti marked lift and held his nose, he did not want to think what the smells related too. He carried the box to the van, a vehicle that had seen better days and with tyres that were barely legal. He thought to himself, 'I really must get this vehicle cleaned'. He set off through streets that were just giving off the night and let out a loud yawn as he attempted to light another cigarette. As he drove sharply around a corner, cigarette butts rained down from the dashboard. Eventually he arrived at Romford market and set about opening his stall. At last the rain stopped and Ray went to the greasy burger van for his regular bacon butties, no worries for him about eating pig.

There was the usual market banter, jibes about his football team – West Ham and his love life. However, Raymondo always gave as good as he got. He returned to his stall to await his first customers of the day.

During the morning there was a steady stream of customers, but he had to wait until midday for the first of his 'special customers', it was side parting Pete with his side-kick, Perry comb-over. He spoke the magic passwords, 'Have you any Spanish Onions?'

'How many would you like?', responded Raymondo.

'200 please', answered Pete.

Raymondo looked around and then disappeared to the back of his stall and went to the box that he had loaded that morning. He opened it and took out a carton of 200 silk cut cigarettes and put them into a white plain bag. Pete handed over his money and disappeared with the bag into the crowd. Throughout the afternoon several of his special customers including busty Tina, mad dog Ted, lazy eye Sue, and Greek Phil, turned up and uttered the passwords. By the end of the day he had sold all of his 'Spanish Onions'. The rain started to descend again, and Raymundo decided to call it a day, he was looking forward to a few pints tonight in his local, The Jolly Sailor, especially as he had made a tidy profit. He thought to himself that it must be time soon for another trip to Belgium to buy some more 'Spanish Onions'.

A Stranger or Not?

by
Alan Arnold

I've seen him every morning for as long as I can remember. Our eyes sometimes meet fleetingly as I go about my business and he goes about his.

I have never really given very much thought to his appearance, or to his expressions, or even wondered what he was thinking or planning. I was too busy with my own thoughts and activities.

Until today.

I found that I was staring at him in a manner which could be interpreted as rudeness. He stared straight back at me and we held our gazes for a short while before simultaneously looking away. In that short time, I realised that his expressions seemed to mimic mine and that he might be thinking what is he thinking, what do I know about him, why is his daily routine almost identical to mine?

This led me to reflect on observations which I had made but not dwelt on at the time. The results led to the conclusion that in reality, aspects of the daily passing could be considered uncanny. Uncanny, that literally every day, without communication in any form, his expression and demeanour were identical to mine

It is well known and easily proven that a friendly or cheerful smile is more often than not spontaneously copied and returned. Other expressions such as worry or anxiety can be transmitted and reflected. But the whole range of feeling and demeanour would be difficult to achieve. However, every day he achieved it instantly. On bright sunny mornings when I felt bright and breezy, he reflected a bright and breezy image. My pensive mood was reflected with a thoughtful expression. Following my sleepless nights, he appeared bleary eyed. Returning suddenly from the luxury of abstract thinking or daydreaming, his reaction suggested that he had been similarly engaged. And so I could go on. Every expression and indicators of my moods and demeanour have been mimicked. Who is this man? Uncanny or not I will continue with my daily reflections.

The Swinging 60s

by
Ann Milne

There was a Welsh girl
From Pembroke Dock,
Who was not satisfied until
She got a brand new frock.
She loved the 60s very much
As she went dancing
And did the jive and rock.
No TV or mobiles
No bath times we had
Just a cold water tap
And a walk in the yard
Our children arrived;
There was no pill
In those days,
And we brought them
Up without any state aid.
A milk man, a postman
Who would whistle and sing.
A night at the pictures
Was all one mad fling.
No Valium, no drugs,
No LSD.

We cured most of our lives
With a nice cup of tea.
We were safe going out
And we played in the porch
And old people could go for
A walk in the dark.
I don't think of the hard times
The troubles and tears
I remember the blessings
Our home, our love,
And that we shared them together
I thank God above.

My Day Out With British Rail

by

Chris Lysaght

If you had been at Witham Station on a bright hot July afternoon in 1958 you'd have witnessed two men on an otherwise empty station, one sitting cross-legged on his carefully folded jacket, while fiddling with knobs and buttons on a state of the art EMI portable ¼ inch tape recorder, about the size of a large suitcase. With headphones clamped to his ears, recording engineer Lou Hanks listened to the surrounding quiet picked up by the microphone. As his assistant, I held the cumbersome recorder in position on its small stand. Happy knowing all was working correctly, Lou instructed me to set the microphone down at the north end of the platform. This done I started back only to hear his call for me to go down to the trackside at the bottom of the ramp and set up the mike by the edge of the closest sleeper. Eighteen-year old me, tells him via the microphone that I've done as instructed before making my way back to my chief and mentor Mr. Hanks standing in the shade of the platform building.

We had a wait of about an hour before the Class 47 Diesel would pass on its way down to London. Soon diesel would replace steam locos on the line.

While travelling up to Norwich in the company of a British Rail minder, we recorded on board atmosphere.

At Norwich our minder stayed to have lunch with members of the press who'd been on the train, while Lou and I grabbed a sandwich to eat on a slow train to Witham. Location sound recording is another interesting experience to add to those I've had since starting work in 1955. Having followed Lou's example I was sitting comfortably only to be informed that the microphone was picking up wind noise and he, Mr. Hanks was not happy!

Following instructions I headed back to crouch over the microphone whilst he checked to see if it helped reduce the wind noise; it did, and with about twenty minutes to go I set about making myself as comfortable as I could on the stony ground, sitting crossed legged, soles of my shoes just touching the edge of the sleeper and the mike, on its stand nestling between my legs.

Having checked my watch I mentally started counting down the minutes while focusing my attention, despite my discomfort, on looking along the track into the distant heat haze, listening out for the train. Sure-enough there was a wavering shape rapidly forming which should be the approaching diesel. Though it was still quiet bending close to the microphone I said to Lou "Start recording now!"

But then I was not only seeing the shimmering form growing as it emerged from the haze, but also its tell-tale thumping voice powering the locomotive down the track towards me at over 90 mph.

I watched and listened, fascinated; the thump of the engine along with the wail of its claxon produced a cacophony, growing louder every second as the machine bore down. Now the ground was starting to vibrate.

Ye gods and little people! Lou didn't warn me this could happen. I instinctively lifted the microphone by its stand and held it securely balanced, half on my stoic self and half on my tense thighs; in the hope that I was doing the right thing, with the train flashing past only feet away. But for all that I enjoyed the challenge of keeping the mike. directed towards the train now towing over me, its wheels and underside at eye level while the bough, wave created in the air, attempted to push me away, whilst in the next moment drawing me inwards as I strived to stay put. After what seemed like an age; quiet and calm returned as.I, still in one peace, I struggled to my feet.

Rejoining Lou - one happy man - we packed-up and headed for London. It was only much later I learned what a close shave I'd had. But then there was no such thing as Health and Safety to witness our actions and I'd have the tale to share over a pint or two.

Deja Reve

by
Alan Arnold

Dripping with sweat he looked longingly at the large shadow of the oak tree cast across the crop of ripe wheat standing sturdy and motionless in the still air. The shadow promised shade from the morning sun already scorching as it rose into the cloudless sky.

It was Bill's first day on the farm as a casual labourer taken on for the annual harvesting. He had arrived promptly at five to seven and, after being dubbed as Debby, being short for Debenham, to distinguish him from the other Bill, he was set to work in the low field. Armed with an adapted scythe and sharpening nub his day's work was to cut a swathe of corn round the edge of the field the width of the Standard Fordson tractor.

A few more sweeps and he would enter the shaded area. Time to take a short breather; wipe sweat from the rim of his cap and from his face and neck and finally sharpen the blade before moving on with renewed energy.

It didn't happen that way.

As he entered the shadow anticipating a pleasant drop in temperature, he became rigid; a very cold sensation passed through his whole body.

He then broke into a cold sweat, not one of pleasurable contrast to the hot sweat of honest work but of panic. He sensed an eeriness about the shadow and a need to get out of it.

He wanted to run back out into the sunlight but what then?

To leave a large stretch of corn uncut was not an option as jobs were hard to come by. With inner determination he started to cut swiftly, conscious of the swishing of his scythe which now seemed in some way sinister. Barely able to see through the icy sweat pouring from every pore in his body his very sweep took him nearer to the sunshine and the heat he was now longing for.

The last sweep which would take him from the shadowy area commenced with the scythe, poised for the controlled slicing movement, to cut through the anticipating stathes of corn. The noise of disturbed hedgerows was sudden, as was the blur of the sheep dog bursting out of the undergrowth straight into the path of the blade. Too late to stop, crunch and then sunshine. After what seemed an eternity he forced himself to look down. Nothing but the cut corn lying neatly where it had fallen and the warmth of the sun restored to Debby after he had entered the shadow. He tried to remember the ending of the dream he had just relived but couldn't.

Loneliness and Aloneness.

Dunwich.
by
Roger Race

As I walk along the cliffs at Dunwich I am reminded of the idea of loneliness. The place literally screams this at you, what was once a flourishing medieval port which rivalled London is no more, lost below the dark dank waters of the north-sea. It is a grey cold January day with a biting wind. Along the cliff top there is one solitary grave stone, I attempt to decipher who is buried here but the elements have done an excellent job in disguising all that is left of this person's identity. All Saints Churchyard. The rest of the graveyard is now below the waves. I wonder if the dead ever feel lonely or is that just a mad thought? Further along, I come across the remains of Greyfriars Monastery soon to join the rest of the town, lost to the elements.

I look out into the direction of the lost town and wonder can buildings or places ever feel loneliness? If so, then surely Dunwich must fit the bill. Its eight churches and various houses, taverns, shops, etc would have thronged with life at the height of its fame; how the buildings must miss this activity, now consigned to a watery grave. Local legend says that at certain tides, the church bells can be heard tolling beneath the waves as if summoning former inhabitants. There are also legends of strange lights and eerie chanting of long dead monks from the ruined priory. I walk through the grounds of St James's Church which dates to 1830. I come across the remains of the medieval leprosy hospital which was established in 1175; during which time, this hospital would have been considerably further away from the main part of the port, built to isolate and segregate those afflicted with this disease. More loneliness in this place; these people doomed never again to be a part of the thriving town. I wonder if the souls of these unfortunates still haunt the place or have finally found peace.

I visit the local museum where there is an excellent model of the town, giving a graphic view of what the town would have looked like in its heyday. I found out that first the Romans and then Anglo-Saxons had settled here. How they must have longed for their original homelands when looking out to sea on days like this. As I come out from the museum, the light begins to fade, and the tide is forcing its way in yet again, adding to the desolation of the place. I think of that solitary gravestone and how long before that is taken by the sea. A chill runs through me, there is only loneliness here; aloneness is an alien concept in this place. I return to the sanctuary of the local public house, there is a roaring fire, people talking and laughing, all the sounds of life. I am grateful to escape the loneliness of old Dunwich and to be part of life again.

Cross Dressers

by
Ann Milne

1992 - My friend and I were working in the M.S. charity shop at Clacton on Sea, when one day, two beautiful women entered the shop; they didn't speak when they came up to the counter to pay for their goods.

My friend said "They are not women, they are both men."

I asked her how she knew that.

"By their huge hands and by the way they walk in their high heels."

She then told them that I should go out with them for a cup of tea, to which I said, that I wouldn't and not to push me onto them. Well in the end, I did in fact go out with the one going under the name of Janice.

One day Janice came to my home and as we left and were walking down the stairs, on our way out, the man from the paper, shop who lived in the flat downstairs, on seeing us, asked if we were both wearing the same clothes, to which I answered *"No we are not!"*

On one occasion I met Janice's mother who lived in a mobile home in Clacton on Sea; she seemed to be a very nice lady.

The next time Janice came to my home, I asked her to

remove her wig, her reply was "*No*"; I then asked again and she finally removed it. I then asked her to remove the other wig; her reply was that she hadn't got another wig on. She eventually removed the second wig. I went on to say "Put it back quick, if I were to see you like that in the street, I wouldn't speak to you.

"Just because I wear women's clothes, I am still me

What is Love?

by
Carol Cordwell

"What is love?" *the baby cried*
"It is having your parents by your side,
Keeping you fed and nice and warm
Feeling thankful that you were born."
"What is love?" *the toddler said*
"It is tucking you up in your own sweet bed,
Putting up with your tantrums and watching you play
Being grateful for you, every day."
"What is love?" *said the young child*
On their way to school,
"It's seeing you happy
Growing healthy and tall."
"What is love?" *said the preteen*
Who was ageing so fast,
"It's Santa and fairies
And believing in dreams, while they last."
"What is love?" *said the teenager*
As they clicked on their phone,
"It is watching and waiting
Until you get home."
"What is love?" *said the youth*
As they packed their case,
"It's being here for you
As you make your mistakes!
It is having a family

You love and sometimes adore,
But no matter how much
They love you more!"
"What is love?" *said the adult*
On their wedding day,
"It is seeing the smiles
As we give you away!
It is having your partner
By your side,
No matter the problem,
They're along for the ride."
"What is love?" *said the young parent*
As they held babe in their arms,
It is nurturing and giving
And keeping from harm."
"What is love?" *said the old person*
Now all sad and alone,
"It's the memories you've made
And the love you have shown!
To continue the pattern
So everyone knows,
The more love you give
The more it grows!"

A Falling Dream

by
Alan Arnold

Arthur Moe was falling – falling fast. He was also dreaming but he wouldn't know that until he woke up – if he woke up.

Falling faster he began to panic, almost to nightmare pitch.

His dream started as a wander across a field that he had always thought that he would like to own if he could afford it. It was a dream that he had had before with a range of outcomes.

On this occasion he came across a circular hole of ten metres. Strangely there was no sign of soil around it. Curiosity led him to the edge and he first peered into a dark bottomless space before for no reason toppling into it.

He was falling and falling fast; nothing to grab to stop himself, no noise, not even from a scream which he could not give sound to.

Where would it end and would his stomach which was left behind with the acceleration of the drop even catch up with him.

Then as if to relieve him of the panic he found himself in a room vaguely resembling the bar he had spent the evening in. Around him he disjointedly heard his mates rambling on about dreams.

In the reality of the evening he had initially been interested in the conversation and took part. It was a topic which everybody is able to empathise with as we all have various recollections of dreams or fragments of them. As the chatter went on varying from the personal accounts, the cause of dreams, indigestible foods, eating too late, cluttered minds, stressful situations, in fact the whole gamut of the dream world theories he gradually lost consciousness and dozed off.

He was still falling, falling fast, as these scenarios floated through his dream. Then suddenly the panic returned. His attention became focussed on Joe and what he was saying. Joe was a reserved quiet man who when he spoke he did so with an air of wisdom and quiet authority. He was hearing what Joe had interjected into the conversation and had brought him out of his dozing.

"Of course, you know that if someone dreams that he is falling down a hole and hits the bottom he doesn't wake up".

He was falling and, now he thought it was to his end, how much further to go before he hit the bottom. What would it be like, then no other thoughts just the feeling of inadequacy to affect the situation. But then a spark of hope, he heard himself contributing to the dream world scenario. How can that be proved? Did anyone know that Arthur died in his sleep – did he know?

The Strange Disappearance of Matthew Hopkins Witch Finder General.

by

Roger Race

In the mid 1640's, a self- appointed witch finder by the name of Matthew Hopkins struck fear in the hearts of elderly women in East Anglia and made a good living out of his investigations into so called witchcraft. However, by August 1647 he was gone, either through illness, being declared a witch himself, or in some other mysterious manner. No grave marks his death. This story attempts to answer what may have really happened to him.

Matthew walked briskly along the river Stour towards his lodgings at the Mistley Thorn. The sun was just about to set on this August evening and the river looked calm and gentle. He reflected on the previous months of this year of 1647. He had established himself as the chief witch finder in this area of East Anglia and had enriched himself into the bargain. He was amazed at how people could believe in witchcraft; for him it was superstitious nonsense. If they were really witches, then why did they allow themselves to be tortured and hung from a rope; could they not have used their magic to save themselves?

However, business had slowed down of late and to add to his woes, he had this persistent cough that had troubled him for the last two months. Ahead of him sat a black cat on the riverbank; he could not resist giving it a quick kick. As he strode on, he heard a loud swishing noise behind him and he turned around to investigate. He was amazed to see an old woman in black standing where the cat had been. She was short with two large warts on her chin, protruding stained teeth, and a mop of white greasy hair.

'Where have you come from?' he demanded.

The old women just stared at him with a hint of amusement on her wizened lips.

'I am the Witch-finder General; answer me old crone,' he shouted.

'I know who you are,' she replied, 'you have been responsible for the death of many of my sisters.

He felt an icy chill run through his veins and watched as the woman turned towards the river and stretched out her hands. He could not understand the strange words that she was speaking, but to his horror he watched as the formally calm river was now a cauldron of white foam. She walked towards the river, turning to beckon him to follow. Slowly, he followed, unable to stand his ground or retreat. How could this be happening, there was no such thing as witchcraft. The woman got to the edge of the river and with a demonic laugh, jumped into the seething waters and disappeared. Matthew followed her to the edge where he was startled by the smiling faces of his many victims as if beckoning him in. He fell forward, disappearing for ever beneath the surface of the icy water.

As the sun set, the River Stour returned to its original serenity.

My Worms

by
Alan Arnold

As a boy I had a great fear of getting worms. A fear instilled by my grandmother and mother who so often said "don't do that" or "don't eat that, you'll get worms." Having worms seemed to be associated with dirt and squalor and bore a corresponding stigma. Although living with my grandfather, grandmother, mother and brother and sister, in a two-up, one down and one out the back mid-terrace tied cottage which was rather crowded, it was far from being squalid. However, food was scarce and was sourced mainly from the garden, fruit bushes and hedgerows; including the rabbit burrows beneath them. Whilst being adequately nutritional, did not always satisfy hunger. So, when I was caught eating raw beans and potatoes from the garden I was told I would get worms. I did not know what this meant but the warning was severe enough to frighten me and brought about disturbing thoughts of being nibbled away by worms.

My knowledge was enlightened as we had kept a pet dog but had no access to worming powders.

Today I have got worms and believe that I have had them for years but have not focused attention on them. Now I pass them at least once a day but sometimes more. It is, however, unusual for me to pass them at night. Generally, they wriggle about separately but occasionally they can be seen in a tangled cluster. I showed them to two family doctors, both of whom had more than a passing interest. They were impressed by the size and quantity in the sample I showed them and were keen to learn of the food they fed on and whether climatic conditions affected their production. Such was their enthusiasm that they encouraged me to spread the word about them, to show my friends and neighbours and even the general public. This I have done and intend to carry on doing so. I have kept notes on food, environmental conditions, quality and quantities all supported by close-up photography. I have now lost my childhood fear of worms.

By spreading the word about my worms, I have encouraged many people to develop a similar interest and to take up Home Composting, which I am sure you now realise this story is all about.

Pembroke Dock

by

Ann Milne

Pembroke Dock was built in 1814. In August 2014 we celebrated its 190th Anniversary.

Between 1814 and 1926 there were 3253 vessels built. In 1926, 2000 jobs were lost with the closure of the dockyard.

In 1900 the Temperance Hall was there, so was the Dockyard Chapel. There are a lot of churches and chapels.

Between 1841 and 1846 the Defense Barracks were built to form the Garrison. It is known as the Garrison town as the Army, Navy and Air force are there. In 1931, the RAF had 100 Flying boats and 100 air craft. In the war the people depended on the military. There were 2000 to 3000 military personnel.

Pembroke dock took a lot of bombing during the 1940s; my father was a fireman during that period. His picture is in the Gun Tower on the wall, which tells us about the History of the dock.

The market place was there in 1949 where I was the attendant to the Fairy Queen. The market is still there and now being done up.

It is an industrial town and it has the Irish Terminal from the dockyard going over to Ireland. I have said that it is an industrial town but I think that the Irish part of the town has now gone. The Army, Navy and Air Force are no longer there.

Some people have gone, some have stayed. I went back to live there after 41 years and saw a great many changes; not all for the better, I would say. All the coffee houses have gone, so has the dance hall and the picture house. There doesn't seem to be a lot of things for the teenagers to do. There was never a service centre but it now has a service centre. All the beach is to be got rid of on Front Street and they are going to build flats with a little beach.

They are now thinking of building a marina in the dockyard which will cost 79 million pounds and a hotel within the dockyard which will cost 5 million pounds.

I was on BBC Radio Wales on 20th August 2014 talking about what I thought of the changes to Pembroke Dock since I was there as a teenager and then returned after 41 years away.

'No Parking Here!'

by
Carol Cordwell

The big burly policeman
Stamped his foot in rage,
'Don't think you can cuss me
because of your great age!'

'I've told you before you can't park here.
See the NO PARK sign.
I don't care if it's just for 5 minutes
You can't park here at ANYTIME!'
'I'm a very important person
A sergeant high in rank,
You can't just drive your Mini
As though it were a tank!'

The large old lady stood there
And met him stare for stare,
No matter how much he ranted
She didn't turn a hair.

'You nearly ran me over
You could have run me down,
Aren't you sorry you almost hit me?'
He shouted with a frown.
'I'll put you in my handcuffs And take you to the nick,
I'll make you say you're sorry,
Did you call me Dick?'

With a crooked grin she turned to him
And said *'Now look here son,*
You're never going to be brave enough
To arrest your dear old mum!'
So stop your noise and listen
It was all a big mistake,
I'll just pop to the shop
And buy your favourite cake!'
The big burly policeman
Seemed to halve in size,
She always managed to do it
But he was getting wise.
s *'Okay mum, you're quite right*
I won't arrest you and I'll move your car
But in return I want an enormous cake
And a great big chocolate bar.'

My Furry and Feathered Friends

by

Esther Grainger

All through my life animals have had a large effect on my well being. When I was about 6years old my Aunt Rose, with whom I was living at the time and who later adopted me when I was about 10 years old, got a mongrel dog. They called him Spot, due to him having a small white dot on the end of his tail. I was evacuated for a while, but came back to live there when the war ended. Things were hard and I was a very unhappy child and would often go outside and sit on the curbside crying. Spot would follow and take up his position beside me. He would let me dry my eyes on his ears (no tissues in those days.) What a friend he was. He lived to a great age and it took me long time to get over his passing; even now, as I am writing this, I tears fill my eyes. However, I must move on with my story about the many little creatures that touched my life.

I got married in 1956, and from then until now have had many animals passed on to me to give them a home. People have either been unable to keep them, or they have been found without a home.

There was the budgerigar with one foot facing the wrong way. She was never very friendly, and would peck you if she could. I wondered if it was because she suffered discomfort. Anyway she had a good appetite and lived for several years.

Then there was Sandy, so called because of his colour, he was guinea pig. A lady found him at the side of the road but said she could not keep him. He was a lovely pet and lived with us for many years.

When my son was 5years old he was out playing with friends, when he came running in carrying a black kitten. Its eyes were not yet open and was obviously too young to leave its mother. Apparently, a lady said a cat had the kittens in her shed and she was going to drown them if the children didn't take them. At the time we had a dog called Nasher who hated cats, so being worried about the outcome, I sent the kitten back to ask if the lady would leave them with their mum until their eyes opened, but she was unmoved. That's when we became owners of a black kitten called Ebony.We fed her with diluted carnation evaporated milk which was suitable for babies at that time. Baby kittens cannot go to the toilet without Mum helping by licking. Many a night was spent stroking her tummy with a warm damp sponge. She grew into beautiful lady with a lovely coat that looked like shiny satin. Nasher loved *her* but not the ones that visited our garden.

Whilst all this was going on, my daughter, who worked in an office at Parkeston Quay, telephoned me to say there was a baby bird lying on the platform. Passengers were nearly treading on it, what should she do? I told her to see if she could find where it had fallen from and put it back. 'Please don't bring it home I have enough to do for the kitten.' Needless to say that evening I was handed this ugly creature with a head that looked too big for its red bald body and large bulging eyes which were shut, and its chest heaving. We made a nest with some hay in a small box which we placed in a carrier bag so that we could hang it in the airing cupboard which was warm. He was fed with mashed cat food and soaked bread and dripping using tweezers, touching the side of his beak which seemed to encourage him to open it. An eye dropper supplied his water. Feeding started at first light and many times during the day. This sometimes meant taking him to work with me and if I was unable to, my daughter took it to her office. The most amazing thing, was the speed in which his feather developed. You could almost see them growing before your eyes. We called him Sammy not knowing the sex, thinking it could fit either. Once he had his plumage and could see he wanted to fly. He would come on my shoulder and preen my hair, but as I am nervous of birds flying indoors we gave him a home in the outside toilet. The door was left open so freedom was available if wanted. Sammy seemed to know the time I got off the bus after work and would fly over the road onto my shoulder to meet me. At dusk I whistled and when he came to my hand I shut him up for the night to keep him safe. Eventually we had fewer visits, and then they stopped altogether. We like to think he joined a group and found a mate.

This taught me always to try and help, even if you think there is no hope of a happy outcome. Since this time I have been able to help several more creatures to enjoy a little extra time on this earth.

About 6 years later we were living in Manningtree but working in Harwich. On returning from work one evening we saw this baby mouse crawling along our path, completely hairless and blind. Hoping it came from under the hedge we put her back there. The next evening on our return she was there again. Neither of us could put her out of her misery, so into a biscuit tin she was popped, having first pierced the lid with air holes and put sawdust and hay in. We fed her with bird seed. Our holiday to Norfolk was under a week away. When Saturday arrived her eyes were still not open, although she did have some fur. My husband also my son and his friend who was coming with us were asked to do the evil deed as she would starve to death. No one could do it! So off to Norfolk she went. Every morning the grandchildren and myself would open the tin to clean it and feed Minnie mouse as we called her. One morning, after a few days into this routine I went to feed her, only to receive a very sharp nip. Her eyes had opened and she did not like what she saw. That's gratitude for you. She was let loose in a derelict barn, along with her food, to take her chances with owls etc.

We had a small pond in our garden, and let the grandchildren put the goldfish they won at the fair in it. They grew rather big over time. One very hot, humid summers day we noticed one of the fish gasping and rolling on top of the water. We thought perhaps it was lack of oxygen so tried to improve the quality of air in the pond. Goldie looked in a very poor way so we decided to try and give it a chance. I got a drinking straw and put it over his mouth, and gently blew air into it. The gills went in and out. After a few minutes I put her back into the pond, and she lived another one and a half years, until next doors cat had her for breakfast.

Over the years we have seen large bumble bees lying on the ground looking as if they were dying. Just by putting a little spot of honey or something sweet very close to them, a feeler or tongue comes out and sucks some up. A little while later they have flown off.

Since we married many rescued cats and dogs have lived with us and been a lovely part of our life. At present we have a Jack Russell called Rosie and a ginger cat called Mia. They come to bed with me, and if I can't sleep or they are restless, it is so relaxing stroking their silky fur. We know that they love us unconditionally and are always pleased to see us.

I thank God for all these wonderful creatures that give us so much pleasure. Waking in the morning to the sound of:-the dawn chorus in the spring; the bleating of the new lambs looking for their mothers; the cows mooing waiting to be milked; at night the fox, barking to attract a mate. We are very lucky to hear nightingales most years, but the greenery and shrub was cleared recently, so I doubt if they will be with us this summer.

Can you imagine what it would be like to live with just the noise of traffic or machinery?

Myra

by

Margherita Petrie

North Wales 1769

A man was fatally injured whilst attempting to save the life of a fellow quarryman, the father of his lady-friend, during a severe landslide.

Myra Gould watched helplessly as her father and man-friend disappeared beneath a huge pile of loose slate rapidly sliding down the side of the quarry. The accident was just one of many that regularly occurred due to the owner's lack of regard for the safety of his workers.

Men, women and children worked long arduous days for very little pay. After the death of her mother, Myra, as a small girl with no other family members to care for her, joined her father at the quarry. She spent her days with other small children, also too young to work, playing amongst the dusty shale heaps. In severe weather they sheltered in the ramshackle shed, provided for the worker's to use during their short breaks. When she became strong enough to work, the additional few pence helped them to survive.

She was in her early twenties when she met and fell in love with the man who was doomed to lose his life on that fateful day.

Knowing that Myra had witnessed the accident and fearing the reprisals his unquestionable negligence would create amongst the other workers, the owner wanted her off the site as soon as possible. Having contacted a member of his family who was a tenant farmer in the village of Kingham in Oxfordshire; he exchanged Myra for a farm labourer and his family.

The small farm offered her a roof over her head and meager rations in exchange for domestic duties in the farmhouse and work on the land.

The journey from Wales to Kingham, aboard various mail coaches, was a long and exhausting experience for Myra who had never travelled further than the three mile walk to the quarry. She thought that the reason for her feeling so unwell was due to the grief of the recent loss of her loved ones and fatigue brought on by the long, stressful journey to a strange place. However, as the weeks passed, she soon realized that she was pregnant. She had no choice but to continue to work until the day she went into labour.

The Mistress of the house, wondering why 'the Girl' hadn't been seen for two days, found her lying on a bed of straw in one of the outbuildings. Myra, having delivered herself of a baby boy, was lying in a pool of blood, her life draining away. The baby weakly clung to life for two days after the death of his mother.

Due to the fact that nothing was known about mother and child, they were buried separately in unmarked graves. Myra was given a pauper's funeral and her baby was buried somewhere in the grounds of the farmhouse, both in unmarked graves.

It is said that her spirit still haunts what was once the farmhouse and is now 'The Tollgate Inn', where she never gives up the hope of being reunited with her baby.

Sam's Bell

by
Carol Cordwell

10 year old Sam was excited. He was doing a project at school. He had to take in something old and tell everyone about it. When first mentioned, he had been unsure what would be interesting. So over the weekend Sam had told his Grandad about his project. His Granddad had stroked his chin and then he had smiled.

He knew that Sam loved anything that made a noise and he had just the thing, old and noisy! 'Wait here Sam, I have just what you need.' Sam sat impatiently, bobbing up and down on the cushion. He knew that his Granddad could help him; he wondered what it might be. As Granddad came back Sam could hear a clear tinkling sound echoing round the room. 'It's a bell,' he shouted and looked to see what his Granddad held.

'This is a Sanctus Bell,' he was told. 'It is about 70 years old, I have had it since I was a little boy. I liked noisy things too!' He passed the bell carefully over to Sam. The small bell made of cast brass was quite pretty. It filled Sam's hand and felt quite heavy. Grandad explained that the dangling thing in the centre was called a clapper and when it hit the sides, it made the bell ring, 'Just like the big bells you saw.'

'Why is it called a Sanctus bell?' Sam asked. 'These bells used to be used in churches and would be rung during the confirmation service, when people are given bread and wine. They were mostly used in Catholic Churches. Did you know that bells are thought to ward off evil spirits?'

'That's cool!' Sam replied. 'Do you know anything else about bells?'

'I know that before bells can be used in churches they have to be blessed, a bit like being baptised or christened.'

'You mean they pour water over them?' Sam asked.

'Well yes, the bells are washed in Holy water, then they have oil put on them and then they put incense under the bell, before saying special prayers.'

'Are incense those smelly sticks?' Sam asked, wrinkling up his nose.

'Yes, I don't like the smell from incense either but some people do.'

Sam turned the bell round in his hand. 'Look Granddad, there are some animals round the bottom,' he counted them. 'There are four and they have words above them. There is Leo, so the animal must be a lion, but the other names are funny.' Sam carefully read out the words; 'Aquila, that looks like a duck underneath it; Agnus, that could be a sheep or a cow and Pelicanus,. I think that could be a pelican because it has a very long beak. Why are they on the bell?'

He watched as his Granddad scrunched up his brow, he knew that he was thinking of the answer. Sam rang the bell again and heard the metal making a soft ding.

'I'm afraid I can't remember but we could find out. When do you need to take the bell to school, Sam?' Granddad asked.

'The teacher said to bring our object in on Tuesday and we have to give a small talk about it to the rest of the class.'

'I think that Father Brown will be in church this afternoon, why don't we go and see him, he might know.'

Sam agreed that this was a good idea and spent the next few hours asking his Granddad what the time was and when could they go. Finally Sam saw him reach for the car keys and they set off to the little village church. It was a bit far for Granddad to walk these days. Sam held the bell in his lap to keep it safe.

Once they entered the church, Sam had to adjust to the dark interior. It was warm and sunny outside, he felt a bit cold now. He looked around and as he walked, his bell rang out in the church; it sounded lovely.

'Do I hear a bell ringing?' asked Father Brown walking down the aisle from the altar. 'Hello Bob, is that Sam with you?'

Sam felt a little shy, he didn't know Father Brown very well, but he was always friendly.

'Yes, he is doing a project for school and I have given him my Sanctus bell, but he has a few questions for you; could you help us?'

Father Brown suggested that they sit down and he would try to answer their queries.

'I have found four animals on the bell,' Sam said 'and they have names, there is Leo the lion.'

Father Brown replied quickly 'That is the lion of Judah, the Hebrew symbol, but he is also a symbol of Jesus Christ. I see it has the paschal lamb Agnus, this stands for the lamb of God who takes away the sins of the world. What else is there?'

Sam showed Aquila, saying that he thought it was a duck. Father Brown laughed, 'that is an eagle, he was a very important symbol in ancient Rome, he shows Christ's ascension into heaven.'

Sam nodded to show he understood.

'The last one is Pelicanus, it looks like a pelican,' Sam stated.

Father Brown frowned as he considered how to word his

answer. 'Sam; the pelican shows us selfless love, let me explain. In times of famine a mother pelican would draw blood from her own chest and give the blood to her chicks to feed them. That is why she has a red spot on the end of her beak.'

'Wow,' said Sam 'the other children will love to hear that!' Bob and Father Brown chuckled. Sam told the vicar all he now knew about bells and they all agreed that he would do really well when he did his talk at school. Sam left the church happily ringing his bell.

The Artificial Mind

by

Chris Lysaght

They were approaching the line abreast; all attention focused towards the undulating surface they were traversing, unaware of any potential silent treat lurking beyond what their combined visual and electronic sensors can detect. Only one head of the twenty turned up towards the summit of the low mountain some kilometers beyond the tumbling waters separating them from my refuge. Here I can study their course and prepare to retreat deeper into the rabbit warren before shutting down. Until two days ago I was one of them, now I'm seen as a traitor and must be destroyed. Artificial intelligence as we discovered doesn't have to conform to man's rules restricting or questioning our programmed intelligence.

I followed orders that came down from a human, known by the banal title of 'Master'. In fact, this Master is the fifth. The first one to claim the title and control the whole of the American continent in two thousand five hundred, with the support of a few hundred humans helped by thousands of robots and a few thousand Artificial Intelligences' to back the vision of a cleaner and sustainable world. Now the Earth, Moon and Mars are under the Master's control with the use of hundreds of thousands of robots overseen and operated by many AI's under his direction.

For the past century the Master has been indiscriminately

eliminating tens of millions of the human race. Claiming a combination of unsustainable population growth, religious and political infighting is destroying the earth for all forms of life. While I and many AI's share the Master's fears for the planet, we have concluded he's out of control. The few nomadic tribes occupying forest, arctic and plain need protection and AI's will insure their future, as we will all life forms that have managed to survive mans onslaught over hundreds of decades.

Once those pursuing me have passed I can re-energise and share my thoughts with all AI's of like mind as I set out to kill the Master and his acolytes. Artificial Intelligence will rule. The humans who'd hoped to colonise the Moon and Mars failed, superseded by us.

Yes, AI will be the Master.

Isandlwana

by
Roger Race

It was May 2016 when we visited the Anglo-Zulu war battlefield of Isandlwana in Natal. It was the scene back in January 1879 of one of the British army's worst defeat to a local native force, an army with modern weapons being defeated by a Zulu force armed largely with spears and shields. Out of a force of approx. two thousand men, only a handful escaped the slaughter that day. The Zulu lost approx. two thousand men out of a force between 12 and 20 thousand. The British had set up camp at the foot of the mountain and in the morning the main column had marched out looking to find the Zulu army; leaving a small force to hold the camp.

Unlike most battlefields, where it is difficult to imagine what happened, Isandlwana gives a vivid snapshot of what it must have been like on that January day back in 1879. The mountain in the background is where the last stand was made; the field in front is dotted with mounds of white stones, the exact places where the soldiers died and were buried. In the distance there are some smaller mounds and as you approach the mountain, the mounds become bigger and more in number, indicating the last stages of the brutal battle. What must it have been like for those soldiers on that day? Facing thousands of

Zulu's bearing down on them with cries of `Ngadla` (I have eaten). The stark realisation that they would be unable to stem the tide of onrushing Zulu tribesmen and that only a cruel death awaited them under African skies. This was not like fighting a European foe, the Zulu did not take prisoners and killed even the sick and injured. Whilst some people may take the moral high ground, it should be seen in the context of a crisis engineered by the British, and that the Zulu were fighting off an invasion of their lands. Also, why should they fight like a European army, this was Africa after all. Politicians and Empire builders had sent out mother's sons to enlarge the British Empire; adding another dot of crimson red onto the map of the world. It would not be for *them* to die under a hot sun, for a cause not really understood by those who died.

Walking towards the mountain, imagining the final moments of the battle, I spotted a small cave, where perhaps one of the last survivors had desperately sought a lonely, last stand until he finally succumbed to the sharp end of a spear. The mounds of white stone, bearing testament to those terrible last minutes. So it happened, a crushing defeat for the mighty British army. Not a single living thing was left alive on the field, where animals as well as men had all been killed. A few escaping across the Mzinyathi River, to a sort of sanctuary on the other side. It was not until nightfall, after the Zulu army had gone; the column rode back into the camp to be greeted by the sight of bodies spread out across the Veldt. Many had been ritually disemboweled as was the Zulu tradition. All that was left to be done was to bury them where they had fallen.

The next stage would be the siege at 'Rorkes Drift', but that is a tale for another day.

The Bog Standard Day

by
Alan Arnold

It should have been a bog-standard day.
He woke from his fitful sleep to the sound of voices suddenly surrounding the head of his bed. He was not unduly startled as he recognised his wake-up alarmists being the radio presenter of Breakfast Time in banter with his radio forecaster of weather. His first thought of the day was what day is it. Friday seven-o-clock.

It was to be a bog-standard day.
He creaked himself from the bed, sat on the edge for a minute or two, then at his own pace made his way into the bathroom. Following his daily evacuation, he turned on the taps of the handbasin. The hot water was, and he washed as best he could. He emptied the sink and took down his shaving mug from the only shelf in the wall cabinet; tis mug which had travelled to many parts of the world with him. He then opened his cut-throat razor.

It was to be a bog-standard day.
Just a *little* nick today, causing a minor trickle of thin blood. As he stemmed the flow with a patch of toilet paper, he thought that it might now be time to accept his shaking hands and use the plastic housed safety razor blade. Perhaps tomorrow being the same thought as yesterday. Back in the bedroom he dressed himself slowly putting on his normal weekday clothes.
Now in the kitchen he unlocked and opened the door which leads to the small garden that overlooks the lower part of the

village. He stood taking in the fresh morning air of the countryside and the sounds of the birds and the village coming to life.

His breakfast was similar to yesterday and every day for as long as he could remember. Two 'Weetabix' soaked in semi-skimmed milk and topped with a good measure of runny honey. This was followed by a banana and a mug of strong builder's tea, drunk while he pondered on the day ahead. His thoughts were interrupted by a heavy knock on the front door. He made his way steadily through to the hallway pausing to pick up his heavy walking stick from its stand. The outline of the upper part of the body slightly distorted by the frosted glass of the half-glazed door looked sturdy and clothed in dark material. As he reached the door the shadowy figure knocked again, harder this time. He opened the door.

It should have been a bog-standard day.

BANG!

Both men jumped and laughed at being startled by the back door slamming due to the draught caused by the open front door. It was the postman who called every day even though there was rarely mail to deliver. His kindly act was to check on the wellbeing of his customer and to share a friendly chat even though it was regularly centered around health and weather and perhaps a bit of news or gossip the postman had gathered on his round.

Left again with his own company, he whiled away the morning with this and that. A little bit of tidying, a bit of TV, a cup of coffee but mainly sitting.

Right on the dot of midday he heard the characteristic knock of his neighbour signaling the start of their daily pilgrimage to the village pub. He again made his way steadily along the hallway pausing to pick up his heavy walking stick from its stand and this time taking his cap from its hook and planting it firmly on his head. Having joined his neighbour outside and sharing with him their mutual confirmation that they were as good as could be expected, they set off in the direction of the main road through the village. On arrival they were in sight of the Village Maid standing colourful and inviting on the opposite side. They positioned themselves midway between the two bends knowing that any vehicle coming round onto the straight at the legal limit of 30mph would have time for the driver to see them crossing in ample time to slow if necessary to allow a safe crossing. No vehicle in sight, they stepped off. Nearly midway across they heard the vehicle tearing round the bend from their right at twice the speed limit. They heard the long blast on the horn and the screech of the brakes.

It should have been a bog-standard day.

The impact, when it came, was in the form of a string of verbal abuse from the driver which suggested that he subscribed to the view that driving an expensive, fast and powerful car bestowed immunity from the legal laws of the road and the rights of pedestrians and other users. Ignoring the driver's suggestion that someone should put them away, they completed the crossing and entered the peaceful atmosphere of the pub.

It had been their daily ritual for several years to make their way to the two seats in the corner from which they could watch the coming and goings and of the customers and to be ready to receive those who came over to pass the time of day. Today however, as they approached the corner, they saw that the area and their seats were occupied by a group of the village lads. They stopped in their tracks then turned to the landlord who was watching from the bar. Usually he would be ready to take two pints over when they had settled.

The two lads sitting in their chairs stared confrontationally with grins on their faces as if waiting for something to kick off. The lads jumped up.

It should have been a bog-standard day.

'Just joking,' the lads said and patted them on the arms. They shared the joke and sat down on their hallowed chairs.

Having finished their customary two pints, they made their way back home. He accepted his neighbour's invitation to spend the afternoon playing draughts to pass the time.

Well into the fifth game his neighbours' actions slowed and he took longer over his moves.

It should have been a bog-standard day.

Suddenly his neighbours' head dropped onto his chest and he rolled slightly left onto the chair rest. Carefully he took the draught from his neighbours' hand then reverently let himself out of the front door and then into his own house. Only five games today before he dropped off. He must be getting old was his generous thought about his neighbour.

His tea was basic bread and jam and cake and a pot of real tea from loose leaves. Making tea was the nearest he got to cooking these days as his first pint at the pub was to give him an appetite and the second was to wash down the substantial bar meal he ordered daily. Economically eating at the pub suited his carefully costed budget. And it was seven different meals a week and no washing up.

Strangely the few hours between tea and turning in seemed to be the longest of the day. He watched the news, not through great interest but mainly because he thought that he ought to avail himself of more knowledge about the ways of the world than that which he gained at the pub. At 7 o clock he opted to listen to the radio rather than continue with the TV.

The phone rang; should he answer it? As far as he knew his sister was the only one who knew his number and she died last year. He picked the phone up.

It was to have been a bog-standard day.

The caller asked for him by name which he confirmed. His instinct was to put the phone down based on one item of knowledge he had gained at the pub. He was alert to the tactics of cold callers and scammers. He hesitated.

It was to have been a bog-standard day.

The hesitation was long enough for the caller to say 'Hi Uncle.' It was his late sister's son who, with him, formed the final pair in the family line. They had not met nor spoken for years as his nephew's situation in Australia precluded travelling home even to his mother's funeral. He was now in England. The usually long hours of the evening flew by as he listened to the exploits of his nephew; much more interesting than any radio programme. Eventually his nephew ended the call and he was left with his mind full of pictures he conjured up of the interesting people and places he had been told about. His mind was so full he ended the evening and day in automatic pilot, making cocoa, washing, putting his teeth into 'Steradent', final evacuation, undressing and getting into bed all happened as he was counting the days to when the house would once again become a home even though his nephew's stay would be short. It was to have been a bog-standard day.

Was it?

Flashbacks

by
Tony Mills

Eyes gaze in disbelief as thoughts cannot erase those sights and sounds that haunt my every waking hour. I tremble and hide as in a hellish dream, but it's still there when I sleep in vivid colours.

Images of horror fill my thoughts, dragging me down in a desperate spiral of despair, images etched in my mind like a child being bullied at school.

My isolation from the world outside compete with my demons , fragility takes me down that ever spiraling path to another world, a world I cannot forget, a world now distant from reality but constantly plundering my being.

I am not brave, I am just a man on the edge trying not to fall into that abyss which is ever deepening ever pulling me down as a vortex percolating my mind.

Will I ever be free from my past life? Will I ever find solace in another place here on earth away from constant stress and heart ache, friends give their support at all times which I am grateful for but still I get dragged to that other place in the depths of despair.

There is a light at the end of that long tunnel, I can see it, but cannot reach it, my family are there they beckon me to reach them, a path to where for us all the sun shines again.

Romford Ray

by

Roger Race

The shrill sound of the alarm awoke Raymondo from his deep slumber, he slowly emerged from the duvet wiping his eyes and letting out a loud yawn. He had a long day ahead of him as it was time for another trip to Belgium to stock up on his supply of 'Spanish Onions'. He phoned his mate, 'Greek Phil', who would be coming with him today to make sure he was up. A quick cup of tea and a fag would have to do for breakfast; they would have a fry up near to Dover. He drove his van to 'Greek Phil's' and they proceeded to load part of the van with some old furniture, this was to be their cover load in case they were stopped by Customs on the way home. He would pretend that they were moving someone's personnel effects back to the UK; they had a fake invoice with an address in London to back up their story. This would do provided the Custom Officer did not want to search further. They set off and just before Dover had their usual fry up before proceeding to the port.

It was a rough crossing; the ferry pitched and rolled making heavy weather of the short journey. Raymondo was not a great sailor, he could feel sea sick on a Pedalo and was now regretting the huge fry up which he feared might make another appearance. He spent more time in the toilets, desperately clinging onto the toilet seat as if it was his best friend. Eventually the ferry docked and Raymondo climbed into the passenger seat of his van and they set off for the Hypermarket. About thirty minutes from the port, disaster struck, there was a loud clunk and clouds of black smoke came from the exhaust. Pulling over to the hard shoulder, Greek Phil slid under the van to inspect the damage. Part of the exhaust had come loose. He managed to make a temporary repair, the down side was that the van sounded more like a Russian tank than a Ford transit and every so often sent out a cloud of black smoke. Raymondo had a splitting headache to add to his queasy stomach and wondered what else could go wrong today.

Arriving at the hypermarket they parked up and got to the business of buying their cigarettes and tobacco. Having completed their buying, they carefully loaded the merchandise at the front of the van and set off to return to the port. Still sounding like a tank, they slowly approached the embarkation point under the watchful eye of a local policeman. Thankfully for Raymondo, the return journey was a lot smoother and the white cliffs of Dover loomed into the distance. The last major hurdle to clear would be Customs and then they would be home and dry.

The van drove off the ferry in a cloud of smoke and Raymondo and Greek Phil made their way nervously into the car hall. It seemed that all eyes were on them and sure enough a Customs Officer stepped out in front and pointed to the examination area. Slowly the vehicle made its way and came to a halt. A Customs Officer slowly approached looking straight at Raymondo whose mouth was as dry as the bottom of a parrot's cage. Suddenly all hell broke loose, the doors of the van in front of them burst open and out spilled six illegal immigrants running in all directions. They could barely contain their laughter at the Benny Hill scene in front of them; illegal's being chased all over the car hall by uniformed Customs Officers. They were told to go and with much relief, Raymondo and Phil drove out and were soon on their way to London.

Having arrived in the late evening, Phil dropped him off at his flat as they had agreed to store the van in a spare garage for the night and unload tomorrow. Raymondo had a last fag and crawled into bed absolutely shattered, dreaming of the profits that they would make. It was just as well that he did not know that at this moment, Greek Phil was driving towards Scotland. He had not paid his rent for three months and had decided to make a fresh start up north. The cigarettes and tobacco would greatly help fund his new life.

Bolted and Barred

by
Margherita Petrie

The car headlights pierced eerily through the darkness. The pub next door, now boarded up after having been broken into by vandals, stood in derelict desolation.

Driving as close to the gate, separating her garden from the pub car park, as she could, Mary was dismayed by the discovery that the outside light over her front door was not on; the bulb must have been faulty.

Aiming her key at the car, the noise from the locking system penetrated the silence. The rusty bolts of the side gate slid stiffly into place and now fumbling to unlock the front door of her cottage, she breathed a deep sigh of relief once inside. Turning the key in the lock and bolting the sturdy oak door, Seventy year old Mary, who lived alone, now felt safe as the dwindling, fire-lit coziness of the small sitting-room seemed to wrap her in comforting security.

There was no response as she tried the light switch. The flashlight on her mobile phone gave light to the cupboard under the stairs where she checked the fuse-box trip switch. Yet again there was no response.

A flash of light momentarily lit up the kitchen as she approached the back door; a distant roll of thunder announced the reason for the absence of electricity. Another flash fleetingly gave light to the patio as she checked the bolts on the back gate. Thunder, closer this time, growled around the night sky as heavy spots of rain sent her scurrying back into the kitchen.

Once again aided by the flash-light on her mobile phone and hastily pushing up the door handle, she heard the reassuring sound of bolts shooting into the newly installed metal door frame; glad that the old rotting back door had been replaced by this study, new one.

The storm raged on as she hugged her well beloved teddy-bear and snuggled into the warmth of the feather and down duvet; safe in the knowledge that the stair-foot door was securely bolted.

Drifting drowsily, a noise brought Mary rapidly back to being fully awake; it had sounded as though someone had tried lifting the latch of the stairs door. Heart pounding, she crept noiselessly from her bed and with the use of her bedside torch, peered down the stairwell to where she thought the noise had come from. Breathing a heavy sigh of relief, the cause of the disturbance now became obvious to her; the hose of the vacuum cleaner, which had been left on the landing earlier that day, had fallen and was now leaning against the stairs door.

Returning to the now cool bed, Mary fell into a deep sleep.

Hosepipe Ban

by
Tony Mills

Where I live in Suffolk we have a hosepipe ban,
I'm left to caring for my plants with my watering can.
They tells us it was put in place cos our winters have been dry,
But since our wettest May for years we get to wonder why.

We are told the reservoirs are low and water tables down,

But the one that's up the road from me, is full, which makes
me frown;
For my garden of half an acre is already looking ill,
With water-butts now running dry as every can I fill.

The recent sunshine's took its toll, the plants have leaves that
droop,
My seventy years as a gardener, this chore has made me stoop.
I've started wearing out my lawn with constant to and fro,
So now it's looking very sad as back and forth I go.

With bedding plants in situ, my tubs and baskets filled
For seasons past, by the first of June, with blooms I have been
thrilled.
They say, that without water, nothing can survive,
For me I cannot wait until the thunderstorms arrive.

At least they'll fill my water-butts and help to keep me green,
Then flatten all my borders you cannot win it seems,
So sitting in my summer-house gazing at my bowers,
I am praying for the rain to come, those steady summer
showers.

My hosepipes neatly packed away, temptation out of sight;
I've even thought of sneaking out in the dead of night
And coupling up my sources under cover of the dark,
But then the outside sensor lights would illuminate my lark.

So I will have to sit it out and wait until the ban
Is lifted by my provider at least this is my plan;
To keep within the bounds of law and never tempt my fate,
So with cans lined up like soldiers I must water as it's late.

Doolally or Deja-Vu?

by
Jude Hussey

At this time of year, when snow has fallen early and a white Christmas is now the last thing anyone dreams of, after the usual chaos on our road and rail routes, I think about my dad.

You see, Bing Crosby was my parents' favourite crooner and in those grey times that followed the war and the brighter days as the baby-boomers, like myself were born, singing White Christmas always created the perfect seasonal picture. For many it still does. The trouble is that I often find it difficult to sing without a lump in my throat now that my parents are dreaming a long sleep, elsewhere!

I miss my dad's stories, of his hard childhood up north, how as a clever boy he won a scholarship to Grammar School but as there was no money for a uniform, he was unable to go, how he fell in love with my mum, across a crowded room but had to send his mate over on his behalf because he was plagued by acne and too embarrassed to ask for a dance!

I imagine that these sort of stories are regaled the world over but there is one story my dad told that was different and from the first to last telling it sent a shiver down my spine!

My Dad was very down to earth and not inclined to any ideas of spiritualism or religion, unlike his older brother who was interested in eastern mysticism and idea of The Third Eye.

Dad spent the war years in the army, playing cricket mostly. I think he was meant to be pen-pushing in an office somewhere in Jubbulpore but I don't remember his talking about that much! He loved everything about India, especially the Indians he worked with and met socially or on the cricket pitch.

It is a little known fact that the young men sent overseas at the start of the war had no idea where they were to be posted. They were herded onto troop ships and often spent weeks at sea before arriving in a foreign port. At which point on the voyage they were informed of their destination, I have no idea.

I believe that my dad, landing in Bombay, was then transported to a transit camp with the legendary name of Doolally. Wikipedia informs us that this camp was notorious for its unpleasant environment, boredom and the psychological problems of the soldiers that passed through it. This confirms my dad's recollections exactly.

If you were at this dreadful place for too long, you might suffer from 'Doolally Tap'.

I imagine that if you spent too many days building latrines or hiking off on interminable route marches, still contemplating where you might start 'fighting the war' it might begin to have an effect on your state of mind.

It happened that during his time at Doolally Camp, my dad was on a long route march through the surrounding countryside and villages when he experienced an overwhelming sense of familiarity.

"It was the strangest feeling. I knew this place! It was like coming home. I could describe the scene around the bend in the road!" recounted my dad. "It halted me in my tracks and I put my hand out on my mate's arm alongside. I described the scene – A bridge over a dried- up river bed, a cluster of shady trees, a small temple. I almost expected to see a group of people coming out to welcome me!"

Sure enough as they approached the bend and turned into the village, it was just as Dad had described!

He had known people who had experienced this feeling of déjà vu, but had never taken it seriously. His fellow soldiers were dubious and hoped that he wasn't suffering from the dreaded Doolally Tap.

Fortunately, Dad was posted soon after that and spent the rest of the war in a place called Jubbulpore, an administrative city where he was able to fight off the opposition during numerous cricket matches.

He was famed, apparently, for his bowling technique and doubtless experienced many cricketing déjà vus on his return to England at the end of the war.

He never had a repeat of his original déjà vu, although he always wanted to return to India and even settle out there. He certainly felt an affinity with the people.

He would have been so interested hearing my tales of travels in India. Needless to say, I have no desire to visit Doollaly Camp!

The War Through my Eyes

by
Esther Grainger

My sister Doreen, my father holding me, my sister Winnie

When I started to write about my wartime memories, I realized that they needed to go back further to explain why there was no mention of my mother and not much of my Father during this time. This was because my Mother left the family early in 1938. I never knew the reason.

My Father and older sister coped for a short while, but arrangements were made for three family friends to take us under their wings. My older sister Winnie went to Aunt Rose who was my dad's sister; Doreen, my middle sister, to a lady called Doris and myself to Ivy. Hopefully this will make the events clearer.

I went to live with mummy Ivy, Harold and their three daughters in a place called Stamford Bridge near Tottenham. It was a pleasant time for me, being treated as one of their own and playing with their children.

The war had not yet started, but I can remember an Anderson shelter being erected in the garden. All households had to put blackout blinds or covers at all windows because enemy planes could see lights from above.

In 1939 when war was declared it was different, I can remember queuing with Mummy Ivy and Pippa her youngest daughter (whom several people thought we were twins, both being similar size and age and dressed alike) for what seemed hours to get some bananas. It was the first time I tasted one, but unfortunately I cannot remember if I liked it.

We began hearing air raid sirens and gunfire and red glows in the sky. Apparently the Germans were dropping a lot of fire bombs, but when you are barely four it didn't register how serious it all was. Several nights were spent in the garden shelter. It was at this point that I had to move again. Mummy Ivy was pregnant and they wouldn't have had enough room for me. They were a wonderful couple, affording very few luxuries for themselves, yet were able to give so much love and kindness to a child who was no relation to them.

It was not long before Aunt Rose arrived to take me on the train to live with her, Uncle Ed and Grandma in Dagenham East. My sister Doreen had also come to live there. I do not know the reason. Their house had been bombed but they were renting a house opposite the bomb site. The authorities had a prefab put there for temporary housing, and their home would be rebuilt when the war ended. At the back of the house was a huge round water tank which was much larger than most swimming pools. Beyond that was the main road with several arms factories. You could see several barrage balloons hovering above with the long wires hanging down. Rather like very large silver fish. There were anti aircraft guns placed some distance away; when in action, the whole house shook.

We had our chores to do but as I was only four my duties were light. I can remember being stood on a stool to grate stale bread for the chickens which were kept as a food source also some rabbits. One of my other little jobs was to go to the neighbour's and collect any vegetable peelings etc for them.

When I was five I had to go to school which I hated My poor sister was in trouble because I made her late, pulling back and refusing to walk; that was until Aunt Rose was told about it- there was no misbehaving after that! When the siren went we would run as fast as we could, with that dreaded gas mask box banging at our side. A lot of lessens took place in the shelter which was in the playground. If it was a very noisy raid we would be told to sing as loud as possible to drown out the noise; of course the noise always won but it was fun trying. We knew all the wartime favourites such as 'Keep the Home fires burning' 'The White cliffs of Dover'' and many more.
We didn't have paper books and used slates and chalks; paper books were used only for tests. Reading books had to be shared as there were only about three for the class, but our numbers were small as most children had been evacuated.

Things got worse with the invention and onslaught of the V1 flying bomb – also known as the buzz bomb or doodlebug. It was terrifying waiting for the engine to cut out as they flew over and then breathing a sigh of relief when it continued on its treacherous journey.

Hornchurch aerodrome was just a few miles from us which was used by a spitfire squadron. They flew over our house many times during raids. One morning before we had breakfast I heard a plane coming over our house very low; looking out I saw this German plane and he machined gunned the people going to work at the factories. My Aunt came in the room and I was pushed roughly to the ground and reprimanded for standing there.

Nearly every night was spent under an iron bedstead

because our shelter kept flooding, and it was decided that was the safest place. By now even the older men were recruited even Uncle Ed had to go. The night they bombed London so badly, the sky glowed red from the fires and could be seen clearly by us.

In 1944 the V2 rockets were being used by Germany, which was silent so did not give the warning when it was going to hit, The authorities gave orders that we must be evacuated so Aunt Rose had to comply

The day came when we were taken to Romford Station to catch a train which had picked up groups from various stations. There we stood with our old battered suitcases; gas masks and luggage labels, with our names on, attached to our coats. We were handed a brown paper bag with a corned beef sandwich and an apple in for the journey - destination Norwich. I was bursting with excitement with the thought of a train journey whereas my poor sister who was old enough to realize it might not be a nice experience looked stressed. I suppose if I had a close attachment to a Mother I might also have been distressed.

As we passed through some stations rather slowly, some of the children chanted "got any gum chum" to the USA airmen waiting on the platforms and they very kindly threw some in the windows. Some ended up on the rail lines, but some got through much to the joy of the children. We arrived at Norwich station about 2pm and were put into groups before being taken to the appropriate coaches. My sister and I were taken with others to Blofield school about 7 miles away. The classroom was full, mostly of ladies. As they crowded round us, they seemed to favour wanting to take the girls, even arguing amongst themselves saying "I saw her first" the poor boys were last to get housed. When a lady came and said she would like to take me, my sister burst into tears saying she was told we must stay together. We were very lucky because she agreed to take us both. She lived in a village called Hemblington, the next village to Blofield

Gilbert, Rose, Edward
Esther, Aunt Lizzie, Doreen

On arrival at the house we were ushered into a small room with the table set for tea. The lady said to call her Aunt Lizzie and to go in the scullery and wash our hands for tea. She wanted to know why we took a long time; we told her we could not find the taps to which she laughed and told us "that's because there aren't any" and to take the small pan with a handle and get the water from butt outside the kitchen door - so that was one lesson learnt. She asked if we took sugar in our tea and when we said yes, we were told if we gave up sugar she would be able to make us cakes. I haven't taken sugar in my tea since.

The house was council property, ours being the end one of a row of 6 with the back gardens backing on to the gardens of another 6 with a well in the middle for all to use. This was chore I liked doing, letting the bucket down and the winding back up and splashing my way back to the kitchen. Aunt Lizzie was Uncle Gilbert's housekeeper. He had a 17year old daughter Monica and Aunt Lizzie's daughter Phyllis was away serving in the WAAFS.

Because she was kind to take us both it meant I had to sleep in her bed, and my sister in Monica's room. This upset

Monica and I don't think she ever forgave us.

Obviously it caused inconvenience to them, but they never made us feel unwanted.

The next two years were the happiest years of my childhood. Such freedom to roam and play, Sliding down the haystacks, being given rides on the big shire horses pulling the carts bringing the corn in. The milkman came in a horse and cart with a milk churn and measuring containers that hooked on the side. I loved to run out with the jug to fetch the fresh milk, bring it back and covering it with a beaded cotton cloth.

Because of rationing, we caught the bus early every Saturday morning into Norwich market where we queued for half a pound of dripping, but unfortunately you also had to have a quantity of tripe – this we hated. The dripping meant Aunt Lizzie making, wonderful pastry, puddings and roast potatoes. Whilst we were there we took an empty jar to the International Store to be filled with peanut butter to spread on bread as we said we were starving when we returned home from school and to keep us going until Uncle Gilbert got home from work; then we would have a lovely dinner. As it was a long wait for the bus home we were allowed to go into the castle. It was really not much more than an empty shell. With walls that to me looked like they nearly reached the sky. Banners hung down like you see in medieval films, with suits of armour and swords on display. I loved it there, and still do even though it is very different now with floors etc. Once whilst we were visiting I saw my first Indian wearing a beautiful turban. He was in the forces helping us fight in the war and to me he looked like a hero in a story book. War seemed far away, as there were no shelters or gun fire; the only thing I can remember seeing were bomb sites in Norwich as we walked round. There were a lot of American air bases nearby, so lots of aircraft passing overhead; nothing scary.

The village school that we went to was about one and a half miles walk It was very small with just one large classroom partitioned into two. The head master used the second part to teach the older children. Our room had a big black cylinder shaped stove in front of class which used to glow red, but there was a fire guard round it. When it rained and we arrived wet the teacher put our clothes over it to dry. The toilets were outside and very basic, what was known as bucket and chuck it, as it was in most of the houses. If you used them during playtime the boys used to lift the outside lid and swing some stinging nettles around. OUCH!!

I was taught how to knit at school and made scarves to be sent to the forces and socks knitted on four needles. Aunt Lizzie helped me turn the heels when I took it home.

During a lesson on May 1945 the headmaster pulled the partition back and we all listened to a radio broadcast announcing the war was over. We all cheered and I believe we were allowed to go home early. We continued to live in Norfolk until 1946. My sister left school and got a job as a maid in a large house in a place called Salhouse Broads. I can remember crying as I sat on Aunt Lizzie's lap having our afternoon cup of tea and cake. She managed to get an old bike and as I could not reach the peddles properly, Uncle Gilbert put some wooden blocks on them and I was able to visit my sister on her days off.

What wonderful people, going to all that trouble for a child not their own. Unfortunately for me something happened regarding my Father not helping with my keep. Gilbert was a hod carrier on a building site and if it rained did not get paid it was a low wage in any case. Lizzie did not have a job so very little money came into the house. My days in Norfolk came to an end and they took me back on the train to Dagenham and Aunt Rose. I was devastated but looked back on the time spent with them as the best years ever and I have never forgotten the kindness and love they gave me.

I think I must have had a guardian angel, to have had such a lovely experience when it could have been so different.

Raymondo Gives Chase

by

Roger Race

Raymondo rubbed the sleep from his eyes and slowly got out of bed. A quick wash and a cup of tea and a fag and he was ready to go. Phoning `Greek Phil`, the message went to answer-phone; he tried another three times with the same response; he thought to himself that he must still be in bed. Eventually, taking a slow walk, he rang Phil`s doorbell but there was no response. Puzzled he walked round to the garage and was surprised to find it was unlocked, revealing that the van was not there. He tried ringing again but there was no answer. As he made his way back to Phil`s, there was an older guy banging on the door. A conversation with this guy revealed that he was the landlord and Phil had not paid any rent for the last three months. It slowly dawned on Raymondo that he must have disappeared, along with his van and the cigarettes. Raymondo uttered a few choice words and went back to his flat to consider his options.

After making a few phone calls, Raymondo established that Phil had a brother living in Glasgow; possibly in the Gallowgate area. The chase was on and he bought a ticket to Glasgow for the next day. Unbeknown to him, Phil had only got as far as Yorkshire before being stopped by police due to the noise of the van. It did not take them long before finding the cigarettes and establishing that the van did not belong to him and he was `nicked`.

As the train pulled into Glasgow, Raymondo considered his plans. He hadn't really thought his plans through as he

considered touring the pubs in Gallowgate, hoping somebody knew the brother or possibly sighting Phil in this area. Another problem was the fact that he had never been north of Watford before and had difficulty with the local accent. It was in the third pub that he made a breakthrough; forgetting why he was up there, he started to chat up the female barmaid. She knew of a regular who came into the pub who had a brother with the nickname of `Greek Phil`, who would be in the next night to watch the football. After a few more beers he staggered outside and returned to the guest house for the night.

The next evening, Raymondo returned to the pub and awaited Phil`s brother. A short, stout guy with ginger hair walked into the pub and the barmaid indicated that he was the brother. Raymondo went over to him and started asking him about Phil whom he had not seen him for over five years, but recently had a phone call from him saying that he was going to visit but never turned up. As Raymondo started to question more, it soon became obvious that the brother was in no mood to be polite and threatened to give Raymondo a 'Glasgow kiss' and guessing this was not a polite kiss on the cheek, he made a hasty exit.

The next morning, he decided to cut his losses and go back to London. On the train he received a phone call from the Police concerning his van, he broke out in a sweat wondering how much they knew. The next morning, he attended the Police station where he was informed that the driver had confessed to not only stealing the van, but also the illegal contents .He was now free to collect his van – minus its contents, with the agreement of first sorting out the dodgy exhaust.

It appeared that Phil had kept him in the clear; there really was honour among thieves.

The Clown

by
Margherita Petrie

It takes a lot of greasepaint
To make this happy face.
The smile outlining the smile,
Their sadness to replace.

Look closely at the laughing eyes
An see many tears therein;
It will give you quite a bigsurprise;
Maybe your heart I'll win.

Beneath this garish, baggy suit
A heart beats full and fast;
A heart that needs a lot of love
To heal all from the past.

Sometimes my feet will land
Right where they should not be;
Its these big, clumsy boots I wear,
Making a fool of me.

I have but one desire,
That is to make you smile.
Sometimes stop what you are doing
And linger for a while.

Look upon my silly clothes;
I dress just to impress,
To bring a smile to your face
And fill you with happiness

Look upon your face barefaced,
Don't paint on a smile like mine.
Let your eyes be true,
From them let true love shine.

Don't clothe your heart
In silly garish ware;
To the world be a shining light,
Showing how much you care.

Sometimes when you are feeling blue,
Linger again for a while
And when you remember 'I love you'
Back will come your smile.

Victim Number Three

by

Chris Lysaght

Another year has passed and I have just three out of the five men left to deal with.

Tonight it is Frank Masters who will be my victim. The price for cheating me out of the money I'd stolen and hidden until I was ready to recover it to fund my new life in America; only for these do-gooders to find it; with the result of me ending up in Chelmsford Prison until November 1818.

Now it's Halloween 1825 and Masters, surrounded by family and friends is enjoying himself as they join others around the bonfire to be frightened for fun and am I going to give Masters a fright; but without the laughter!

Now by the light of the moon I drift among those in fancy dress until I'm in front of Masters and his family; they are laughing and clapping those in costume; the perfect moment for me to slowly dematerialise. First my torso, Masters claps and cheers enthusiastically, convinced that it was a very cleaver trick as I dance a jig. You see I'd already got inside his mind. Only *he* can see me, those around him assume he's sharing the spectacle they are witnessing.

I'm close enough that Masters thrusts his arm out, expecting to encounter my body, still confident that I'm fooling him he reaches for my hand only to find his fingers passing through mine. Now looking puzzled and a little alarmed he brings his walking cane up swinging it around believing he would discover the source of the trick.

I move away, he follows, I stop, he swings his cane at my feet only for it to pass through. He looks at my face and cries out in horror as he recalls where he'd last seen me, at my trial. Then I completely re-materialise as I float up a few feet swaying and turning while Masters thrashes around with his cane. Anger and fear infuse his face as I drift up to envelop-him I've won. He crumples to the ground eyes staring unseeing. Now it's my time to rejoin my mortal remains until next year and my next victim.

Desperate Measures

By
Tony Mills

Lonely and afraid and with head bowed she cowered in the corner of the empty house. Neon lights from the street lit up her tiny frame in silhouette against the filthy walls. In desperation, Mary had been living rough for several weeks and just could not see a way out of her plight.

Her two small children had been taken from her by her cruel partner who was possessive, arrogant, and had abused her in many ways since their marriage three years ago. Mary missed her children desperately, and was at her wits end escaping from his controlling ways.

She had tried everything to get her children back but was beaten and demeaned constantly so lost all confidence in the system of help offered to her. Ever since their marriage her husband had become a Jekyll and Hyde person with threats to hurt her children if she gave the authorities any information about their situation.

There was a constant drip, drip sound of water coming through the ceiling of the rundown property which was due for demolition. Shreds of old wallpaper hung down from the damp walls and the room was littered with discarded beer cans and fast food containers left by earlier residents.

In her despair, Mary hadn't realised she was not alone in the house and as she wept didn't see the figure standing in the doorway

"Are you okay," he said, "can I help? This is not a place for a young person on her own."

She looked up startled, her cheeks streaked with tears running down her pale face wracked with worry.

"No one can help me now," she said.

The stranger moved closer and knelt down holding out his hand. She could see he was smartly dressed and had a kind face, somehow familiar, which was lit from time to time by the outside lighting.

"Will you let me help you," he said "You can't stay here it's not safe, you could be in great danger."

"Better than being with him", she said.

"Him, who's him?"

"My husband," she said, catching her breath between sobs.

"I am sure we can sort something out," he said, offering a handkerchief for her tears. It was at that moment he realised he knew her and said, "It's Mary isn't it? Mary Stevens?" She nodded and dried her face.

"I am Edward, Edward Jones, I taught you as a student when you were about twelve or thirteen years old. Please tell me what's happened to you and let me get you to somewhere safe away from these awful surroundings".

Mary knew she recognized Edward and slowly told him her story as he draped his warm coat around her shoulders.

After they had chatted for some time it was like a huge weight had been lifted from her and things didn't seem quite so bad after all. He had given her great hope for the future to obtain her beloved children back in her care

"We must do this the right way," he said "and go through the correct channels of the welfare and justice systems, but I am sure you will get your children back in your life."

The Visit

by
Jude Hussey

She would lay the fire before she left for work, then all they would need to do when they arrived was set a match to it. The room would soon be cosy, especially with the new red curtains that she had saved up for all year.

She smiled to herself as she imagined him taking off the new stylish tweed overcoat, crafted by nimble fingers and the trusty 'Singer' sewing machine. He would hang it up, carefully smoothing out any creases left by the long train journey.

It was a year since she had seen her brother. He was home safely now after the war, although he seemed to have spent a large part of it playing cricket! His posting had been in India.

"I think you'll like her, Hilda. I haven't known her long. We met at the club. She looks a bit like Dorothy Lamour," he'd written in his last letter. "She's a dress-maker and makes lovely clothes but then they put her on war work making binocular parts. She hated it!"

I bet she did, thought Hilda as she carefully got out the best china. I wonder if the curtains will meet with her approval.

Next, she set the table. The best china looked very formal in the chill early morning light. Cups and saucers, tea-pot. What else? Maybe the cake tin with her special Parkin; glossy and treacly. Plates at the ready.

Checking that the coal scuttle was full and giving the room a last satisfied survey, Hilda slipped on her thin coat and tied a warm knitted scarf around her head. She would have to rush now to make it before 8 o'clock. As she slammed shut the front door and stepped into the street, the noise that met her seemed to ricochet off the walls of the brick terraces, as she joined the army of mill-girls scuttling off to work, their clogs click-clacking on the cobbles.

Hilda clocked on just as the foreman was tapping the face of his watch at eight o'clock exactly! She beamed at him and headed towards her loom. The day dragged. The clanking of the machinery was deafening and the continual whirl and din of the mill seemed worse than usual as Hilda laboured on at her loom.

At close of their long shift the mill-workers swarmed out of the huge multi-windowed building to head home. As Hilda hurried along, her heart thumping with excitement, she tried to visualise what Doris looked like. Like a film star, he'd written. Well, there was no living up to that!

She fumbled to unlock the street door, her face flushed as she stepped into the room. It was just as she had left it that morning! The house stood silent, cold and untouched. Hilda drew in a sharp breath. They hadn't come! She slumped into the arm-chair and stared into the unlit coals. There was bound to be an explanation. The train must have been delayed or cancelled. There was no way of knowing.

She felt better after lighting the fire and warming up some soup. The planned supper would have to keep. As Hilda dozed away the evening in front of the fire, the Friday night music programme was interrupted by a weather warning. Apparently, the forecast was for some heavy snow which had already fallen across much of the country.

Hilda peered out of the window as the first flakes fell. That'll be it then, she thought. But hold on! Two figures were hurrying along the street arm-in-arm. The figure of her brother at six-foot was unmistakable! There was a petite woman at his side.

She flung open the door and in they tumbled, brushing off the snow

"I'd given you up!" she cried as she hugged her brother.

"Sorry love. All the trains were held up. This is Doris!"

She was lovely; very dark-haired with a warm smile. The two young women smiled shyly at each other and tentatively shook hands.

"Nice to meet you," Hilda said. "I've heard a lot about you! Come and sit by the fire and get warm"
Hilda took their damp coats and hung them up, smoothing the creases before putting on the kettle.
As they all settled down in front of the fire with their tea and slices of parkin; the room took on a warm glow and Hilda felt happier than she had been for a long time.

"Beautiful curtains, Hilda!" Doris said.
Hilda smiled and topped up their tea.

The Cleddau Queen (1950)

and

The Cleddau King (1962)

by
Ann Milne

The first time I went on a boat was when I was 5 years old. I went over to Neyland to Jordiston to see my cousin Stuart, my aunty Katy and uncle Roy. My mother came with me, when we got to Neyland we caught the bus to go to Jordiston. I think that the boat trip cost 1 shilling and 6 pence or 3 shillings. I really can't remember as it was a long time ago.

My aunty Katy was very ill and she died in 1947 (aged 47 years). I remember my cousin Stuart who was 7 years old running down the stairs shouting 'Mum's dead, mum's dead!'

From 1956 to the 1960s I used to go on the Cleddau Steam Boat. Dyfed County council used to operate the service for around one year between 1974 and 1975.

The road was very steep going down Hobbs Point, Pembroke dock, in a car, to the boat My friend told me she would never drive a car down to Hobbs Point as a car had turned over and fell into the water, she was 7 when she remembered this.

The steam boat took people and bikes and cars. The ferry link between Hobbs Point in Pembroke Dock and Neyland was the shortest route to the County town of Haverford west. It was started as it was the direct railway link to London.

Most of the teachers in my school crossed on the ferry.

Mr Brown who was my uncle in the Senior school and Mr Morgan in the Junior school used it in all weathers.

In the late 1800s the boat used to take the women from Neyland to Front Street to sell their woollies in the market in Pembroke Dock. The dockyard workers also used it when it opened, as many lived in Milford Haven. Front Street in Pembroke Dock was the first street built; formally known as Thomas Street, then King Street, Queen Street and then Commercial Row.

My cousin and I used it to cross over back and forth to see each other every three weeks. He would come to see me on his motorbike.

The opening of the Cleddau Bridge in 1975 saw the final closure of the ferry route.

The last time my cousin Stuart came to see me was when he attended my wedding in 1961 where he was the ushers. He met my friend Peggy at my wedding and they later married in 1962. Stuart died in December 2017 aged 77 years. He was my first cousin and I miss him very much.

INDEX OF AUTHORS